Franklin Fibs

To Cameron, Lauren and Katie — PB

To my son, Robin — BC

Franklin is a trade mark of Kids Can Press Ltd.

ISBN 0-590-44647-9

30 29 28 27 26 25 24 23 22 21 20   9/9 0 1 2 3 4/0

Printed in the U.S.A.   23

First Scholastic printing, February 1992

Franklin Fibs

Written by Paulette Bourgeois
Illustrated by Brenda Clark

SCHOLASTIC INC.
New York Toronto London Auckland Sydney

FRANKLIN could slide down a riverbank all by himself. He could count forwards and backwards. He could zip zippers and button buttons. He could even tie shoe laces, but Franklin could not swallow seventy-six flies in the blink of an eye.

And that was a problem because Franklin said he could. He told all his friends he could. Franklin had fibbed.

It started with Bear.
Bear boasted, "I can climb the highest tree."
He scrambled to the tip of a pine.

Then Hawk bragged, "I can fly over the berry patch without flapping my wings."

He soared over the woods and past the berry patch without ruffling a feather.

Beaver crowed, "I can chop down a tree with just my teeth."

Beaver gnawed first on one side, then on the other. Chips of wood flew this way and that. The tree crashed down.

"And," she said, "I can make my own dam."

Franklin couldn't climb a tree. He couldn't chop down a tree. He couldn't fly. And he forgot everything he *could* do. So he fibbed.

"I can swallow seventy-six flies in the blink of an eye," he said.

His friends were astounded.

"Watch me," said Franklin.

Franklin gobbled two, four, six flies.

"There!"

"But that was only six flies," said Hawk.

"There were only six flies flying," said Franklin. "And I ate them all in the blink of an eye. I could have eaten seventy more."

"Let's see," said Beaver.

Franklin frowned. There was no way he could eat seventy-six flies in the blink of an eye. No way at all.

Franklin had no appetite at dinner.
"What's wrong?" asked his mother.
"I can't eat seventy-six flies in the blink of an eye."
"Neither can I," said Franklin's father.
"Neither can I," said Franklin's mother.
"But you don't have to," said Franklin sadly.

"And I do." Franklin told them all about the flies. His mother nodded and his father hmmmmed.

"You have quite an imagination," said Franklin's father.

The next morning, Franklin's friends were waiting.
Beaver had a surprise.

"Eat them," she dared.

Franklin wrapped a woolly winter scarf twice around
his neck. "Can't," he squawked. "I have a sore throat."

His friends laughed.

Franklin felt terrible. He couldn't eat. He couldn't sleep. He couldn't think of anything but flies and lies.

"I could practice until I *could* swallow seventy-six flies in the blink of an eye," Franklin told his father.

"You could, but it would take a long time," he said.

"I could stop playing with my friends," Franklin told his mother.

"You could, but you might be lonely," she said.

"I could tell them I fibbed," said Franklin.

"You could do that," said Franklin's parents. "And then you can show them what you *can* do."

The next day, Franklin's friends were waiting.

"I can't eat seventy-six flies in the blink of an eye," admitted Franklin.

"We guessed," said Bear.

"But," said Franklin, "I *can* eat seventy-six flies."

Franklin's friends sighed.

"Really," said Franklin.

Franklin ran home.

He got the flies, a bowl, some flour, milk, eggs and honey. He poured and stirred, rolled and baked. Finally, he was ready.

"Watch me!" Franklin gobbled the entire fly pie.
"There," said Franklin licking his lips.
"Amazing! What else can you do?" asked Beaver.
Franklin swaggered with success. He was about to
say that he could eat two fly pies in a gulp.

Then he thought twice and said nothing at all.
Even a turtle gets tired of eating fly pie.